As Long as the Rivers Flow

As Long as

the Rivers Flow

Larry Loyie

with Constance Brissenden

Illustrations by Heather D. Holmlund

Groundwood Books
House of Anansi Press
Toronto Berkeley

*To my family and all young people who seek to know
about a way of life that is fast disappearing.*

In 1944, Larry Loyie, who was then known as Lawrence,
was ten years old and living with his family near Slave Lake
in northern Alberta, Canada.
    This is his story…

THE BABY OWL blinked its round yellow eyes at Lawrence, and the boy blinked back. Peering out from Papa's knapsack, the owlet was a fuzzy brown-and-white bundle. When it saw the people, it let out a demanding "Cheeep" and loudly clacked its beak.

The children jumped back, then laughed. Little sister grabbed at the fluffy feathers.

Papa spoke sternly, "Be careful, Maruk. This owl is just a baby but it is very hungry and its beak is already sharp."

Maruk quickly pulled her hand away.

Papa continued, "When I was out checking my trapline, I found this bird at the bottom of a tree. There were no other owls around, so I picked it up and brought it home. It is a wild thing but it needs us now. Otherwise it will die of hunger or be eaten by a coyote. You children must care for it. Don't give it butter and jam. Feed it wild meat until it is big enough to return to the forest."

"We can keep it in the shed," Lawrence said. "It's always dark in there."

Papa nodded at his eldest son. Lawrence was small for a ten-year-old boy, but he was already wise in the ways of their people.

"I'll fix a place for it to roost," Papa said. Carefully, he carried the owl to the shed. The children crowded around him.

"It can sleep in my old dolly's bed and use the blanket," said Maruk.

"That's a good idea, too." Papa smiled. "Now, my children, you must give it a name."

"Is it a boy or a girl owl?" asked little brother Buddy.

"I can't tell for sure," Papa said. "I think it's a boy."

They all fell silent, thinking of a good name.

"Let's call him Minos," shouted baby brother Leonard.

Minos meant cat. Everyone laughed.

"Let's call him Ooh-Hoo," Lawrence said.

"Ooh-Hoo means owl in our language," said Papa. "That makes it a good name."

Every day the children took Ooh-Hoo pieces of uncooked rabbit meat to eat. They cleaned the shed and filled the water dish. They chased the dog away when he got too close.

After supper every night, Lawrence put on Papa's old moose-hide gloves and went into the shed. At the sight of him, Ooh-Hoo raised his voice and clacked his beak. He seemed to know it was time to play.

One night, Lawrence carried Ooh-Hoo to Mama's clothesline, with the other children following behind. Sitting by the fire, Grandma and Grandpa watched the parade pass by.

Grandma said to Grandpa, "Mosoom, that owl is getting bigger every day."

"I wonder if he will ever leave the children?" Grandpa replied.

At the clothesline, Ooh-Hoo gripped the rope with long, feather-covered claws. He flapped his wings as if to say, "Look at me. I'm big now, too."

In a flash, the little owl was hanging upside down from the clothesline, his wings still flapping. The children jumped up and down with joy. Ooh-Hoo never tired of playing this game. He needed the exercise to strengthen his wings.

When Lawrence put him on the ground, Ooh-Hoo's ear feathers stood up. Lawrence knew he was angry.

Grandpa walked over. "Ooh-Hoo wants to play some more. Toss your owl up in the air. See what happens."

"He might fall and hurt himself," Lawrence said doubtfully.

"Try it. He has been exercising those wings a long time."

Lawrence picked Ooh-Hoo off the ground. Hesitating, he looked down at the owl in his arms. He swung his arms upward and tossed Ooh-Hoo as high as he could.

Ooh-Hoo looked surprised to find himself in the air. He flapped his wings furiously. For an instant he stayed aloft. Then slowly he fluttered to earth.

"He's flying down instead of up," Little Buddy squealed.

Maruk stroked the owl on his head.

"Poor little Ooh-Hoo. You don't have a mama and a papa to teach you how to fly."

ALL afternoon, Mama smoked a moose hide over the smoke pit. Now she took it down from the smoke rack and gave it to Grandma.

"Kokom, here is more hide for those winter clothes you want to make," she said. Lawrence sat and watched his grandmother sewing winter moccasins. The needle in her small hands went smoothly in and out.

Papa and Grandpa were at the barn working on the wagon. They checked the wheels carefully, putting grease on the axles. Uncle Louis oiled the buckles on the horses' harnesses.

"Lunch is ready," Mama called. Inside their log house, they ate moose stew and fresh bread.

Grandpa sipped his tea. "We will soon leave for our summer camp near the river," he said. "The wagon is ready for travel."

"I want to take some vegetables on this trip," said Mama. "And Kokom has canvas tarps for drying berries."

"Do we take our tent?" asked Lawrence.

"Not this time," Papa replied. "The weather is hot and dry. We can make a lean-to for sleeping."

The younger children ran outside to play. Lawrence stayed with the older people, listening carefully.

Mama spoke quietly. "Kokom keeps hearing that children are being taken from their families and put in a school far away." She looked at Lawrence, then lowered her voice even more. He could only hear part of what she said. It was something about prison.

"What are they going to do to us next?" Grandma said.

Lawrence didn't understand. What was this school? He didn't want to leave home. He played with the other children all day. He was learning to hunt and fish to help feed the family, and he was pretty good at it, too.

That night as he lay in bed, he remembered Mama's words. What did they mean?

THE sun was rising as Lawrence slipped out of bed. As always, Grandma and Grandpa were already awake.

"Why are you up so early?" Grandma asked.

"I'm going fishing, Kokom." Lawrence took some hooks and fishing line. At the creek he would cut a fishing pole with his pocket knife. He also took a small frying pan and a piece of bannock.

As he walked along the forest path, he heard a squirrel chatter. To Lawrence she was saying, "Get out of my way! I'm gathering nuts for winter."

An eagle swooped overhead, looking for breakfast.

"You leave my owl alone," said Lawrence.

He smelled wild mint in the air. He would pick some for Mama on his way home.

Lawrence came across some bear tracks. His grandpa had told him that grizzly bear claw marks were deeper and wider than a black bear's marks. The tracks Lawrence found had been made by a black bear, but they were old and dried out.

At the creek, Lawrence caught enough fish to feed the family that day. As he ate his breakfast of fried fish and bannock, he thought of Uncle Louis. Everyone said Uncle Louis was the best tracker and hunter they knew.

Already his uncle had taught him a lot. Once, when they were out in the bush, Uncle Louis had pointed to some half-chewed leaves. "Look at this," he had said. "A moose was here less than an hour ago."

"I want to know as much as Uncle Louis," Lawrence said to himself as he walked home carrying his heavy catch of fish.

BEFORE leaving for their camp, the family laid all their supplies on the ground to see whether anything had been forgotten. There were pots and pans for cooking, and pails for water and berries. A large ax and a small hatchet lay nearby. The sacks would be used to carry dried berries and dried meat. Warm wool blankets were wrapped in a tarp to keep them dry.

"Let's get the rest of last summer's vegetables out of the root cellar," said Mama. Lawrence followed her under the house. It was cool down there, and that kept the vegetables fresh. He held open a sack. Mama put in turnips, onions and potatoes from her garden. Lawrence carried them up for her.

"Now we're ready," Mama said.

Uncle Louis hitched the team of horses to the wagon and drove them to the supplies.

"Whoa, Blackie and Nellie," he commanded in a loud voice.

Mama supervised the loading of the wagon. "Let's put the grub box some place handy so we don't have to dig for it when we get hungry," she said to Papa.

Soon everything was neatly loaded for their two-week stay in the bush.

The little ones were crying because they wanted to go, too.

Lawrence told Maruk, "You have to stay with Auntie Jenny and look after Ooh-Hoo. Don't forget to feed him every day. You know how hungry he gets."

"I know that already," Maruk said in a huff.

Grandma and Grandpa sat on the front seat of the wagon with Mama. Grandpa took the reins. Papa and Uncle Louis set out ahead on foot to clear the trail of any trees or branches that might have been blown down by the wind.

Lawrence slipped into the shed to say goodbye to Ooh-Hoo.

"I wish you were coming," he said.

THE camp road was narrow. Trees crowded in on both sides, sometimes forming a canopy above their heads. A few hours down the trail, Grandpa stopped to rest the horses.

Another wagon pulled up. Auntie Rose, Uncle James and cousins Clara, Leo, William and Sammy had arrived. Sammy, the youngest, was Lawrence's age.

The children walked behind the wagon, telling stories and jokes. They laughed and teased one another. A couple of dogs walked with them.

"I hear you have an owl," said Sammy. He pointed to a shaggy dog with one ear longer than the other. "My dog can do tricks. He can roll over. He barks when I tell him to speak," he boasted.

"My owl is very smart," Lawrence said. "He flies upside down on the clothesline. He's tough, too. He eats raw rabbit."

"But you can't keep him," said Sammy.

"You're just jealous," Lawrence blurted out. "He's ours anyway until he flies away. Ooh-Hoo will always remember us."

He gave Sammy a shove and walked away.

Every year the families camped at the same spot beside a wide river.

When they arrived, Uncle Louis told the children, "Give the horses a good rub-down, then water them. When you finish, go in the bush and haul wood for the fires. Then you can go swimming."

Lawrence and Sammy led the horses close to two tree stumps. They stood on the stumps to rub and brush the horses' backs. Clara, William and Leo looked for wood.

After their chores were done, they raced each other to the river. They had a great water fight, then lay in the sun to dry.

As each family set up a lean-to for sleeping, Grandma and Grandpa gathered spruce boughs for the beds. They laid canvas tarps and blankets over the boughs.

"Spruce boughs keep the frogs and mice out," said Grandma. "They don't like the prickly needles."

Lawrence found it hard to sleep. He could hardly wait for morning. He wanted to pick berries, fish and go swimming all at once.

Far away he heard the sound of an owl hooting. Nearby another owl answered. He fell asleep thinking of Ooh-Hoo.

In the morning, Mama, Grandma and the children walked to the berry patch. Along the way, the children picked small but tasty saskatoonberries. After they had filled their cups, they dumped the berries into big buckets.

"Help me make the berry racks, Lawrence," said Mama. Every year they used the same spruce poles to make the racks.

With Mama's help, Lawrence wove willow tree branches between the poles to make a table. They laid a tarp on top, spreading the berries out in the hot sun. "Turn the berries over," Grandma told cousin Clara. "We want them to be dry by tonight."

Lawrence walked back along the rolling hills to the berry bushes. Sammy shouted, "I bet I can fill my cup faster than you."

The boys picked faster and faster. Lawrence remembered the good patches from the year before. Soon he had filled his cup.

"I win," he yelled and raced toward the buckets. In his haste he tripped over a tree root and went flying. His berries scattered everywhere. His elbow was scraped raw.

His cousins laughed at him

until Mama chased them away. Then she put her arm around him.

"Are you all right?" she asked gently, wiping his elbow with a cloth. Her smile made him strong again.

"Mama," he asked, "am I going to school soon?" He really wanted to know why Mama and Grandma looked so sad and worried, but he didn't know how to ask.

Now Mama frowned. "Don't worry about the school. Just keep picking berries. And remember, slow down next time. Don't pick any more berries for the mice."

DAWN touched the sky. Wisps of mist floated on the damp ground.

"Papa, can I go hunting with you this year?" Lawrence stood as tall as possible when he asked.

Papa shook his head. "Not yet, my son. When we're in the bush, we spread out and walk for miles looking for game. If we're too far from camp, we stay overnight. We take only one blanket each. Your mama wouldn't like you getting cold or sick."

Lawrence looked at the ground to hide his disappointment.

"While we're away, why don't you test your skills?" Papa said. "There's a family of beavers living in the river. They come up for food early every morning and late in the evening. If they smell you, they will dive down and go somewhere else. See if you can fool them."

"I can fool them, Papa."

"Don't be so sure until you try it."

Papa, Uncle Louis and Uncle James picked up their pack-sacks, waved goodbye and disappeared down the trail.

Grandpa told Lawrence, "To see a beaver, you must find a

bushy spot near the river. You must have a clear view of where the water is dark and deep. Look carefully for a nose above the water. That is how beavers check for danger."

In the late afternoon, Lawrence walked to the beaver dam. He chose a spot that looked right, then sat and waited. He heard the buzz of a horsefly and shuddered to think of its painful bite.

Suddenly he remembered his grandma's trick. With his pocket knife, he cut a willow branch to use as a fly swatter. The beavers would think it was the wind blowing.

As he waited, he thought of Mama's delicious rabbit stew cooking on the campfire for supper. His stomach grumbled with hunger. His mouth was dry and got drier as he watched the river.

Now he understood what the hunters meant when they talked about patience and discipline. It would be easy to go back to camp, eat supper and go to bed. But he had to stay to prove himself to his father.

A speck of dark appeared on the silvery water. Ripples followed behind it. Lawrence's heart beat faster. Would the beaver smell him or see him? A long time seemed to pass as he sat motionless. Then the beaver swam to the opposite side of the river, unaware of the boy nearby.

Lawrence had fooled the beaver.

Chapter 3 | **Grizzly!**

LAWRENCE was almost as tall as his grandma. Sometimes he wondered exactly how tall she really was. She always seemed to be bending down, reaching for her sewing or putting a log on the fire.

Her best friend was Whiskers, her dog. He was a rusty brown color. Many long hairs grew on each side of his nose. When he was a puppy, Grandma wanted to call him Wapoose, which meant Rabbit, but she chose Whiskers instead. Wherever Grandma went, Whiskers was not far behind.

Grandma knew just about everything. When she was young, she had been a bronco buster and had ridden horses every day. She could hunt and fish better than most.

"Your kokom is equal to anyone," Papa once told Lawrence. "You will learn a lot from her if you watch and listen."

Listening to Grandma was fun. She talked to the birds, scolding them if they were too noisy. If she heard the howl of a coyote or a wolf, she wondered out loud if it was hungry or lonely. At night she told funny stories until the children fell asleep.

"Today we have to walk a long way," Grandma told Lawrence one morning. "The special medicines I want to pick are on the other side of that big hill. Make sure you pack enough lunch so we don't get hungry."

Lawrence took a gunny sack and packed their lunch. He slung it over his shoulder.

"I'm a real hunter now," he pretended. "I'll bring home lots of food to feed everybody for lots of days."

Grandma turned and looked back at him. "Hurry up, Lawrence. Quit your daydreaming. You're lagging behind."

Under her arm, Grandma carried her small, single-shot .22 rifle. It was so old that it was held together by a bit of wire. Her eyesight was dimming, but she could still bring home a rabbit or partridge for supper.

"My rifle is as old as I am but that doesn't matter. It has kept me in food and clothing for many years. That is all that counts," she said.

Some medicines grew in swampy areas. Others, like sage, grew in dry areas.

"You will find Labrador bushes in the muskeg," Grandma told Lawrence as they walked. "We make tea with the leaves. It helps us feel better when we're tired or feeling sick."

By the shore of a little lake, she used her knife to cut the roots of a plant. From her pouch, she took a pinch of tobacco.

"This is how we give thanks to our mother earth," she said. She put the tobacco in the ground where the root had been.

Grandma held up a chunk of root. "When it is dried, this rat root is good for a sore throat or a cold. Chew a small piece or make a tea with it. I always carry rat root wherever I go."

She knew her grandson was tired, yet he didn't complain. She pointed to a clear stream that gurgled on its way to the river.

"Here is a good spot for a cup of tea and some bannock." Soon her fire burned brightly and the water in her tea pot bubbled. She threw a handful of mint leaves into the pot.

Whiskers eyed the bannock hungrily. "You should be hunting your own food," Grandma told him. Whiskers wagged his tail. Grandma chuckled.

"Take this piece of bannock, you lazy dog. But I expect you to keep your eye out for bears."

"WHERE is Whiskers?"
As Lawrence poured water over the fire, Grandma grumbled out loud. "It's not like that silly dog to run off. He's usually afraid of his own shadow."

She pointed up the trail. "The medicine I want grows just over that hill." Carrying her packsack, she set off quickly with Lawrence following right behind. Their willow branch fly swatters made the only sound in the forest.

Grandma slowed down.

"Something is not right here," she said. "All the birds are quiet."

Lawrence looked around. The forest was still. Even the leaves seemed to have stopped rustling.

Suddenly he felt afraid.

Grandma stopped walking. "Stay behind me, Lawrence. Don't make any noise. Keep a sharp lookout," she ordered.

Lawrence's thoughts raced wildly. He knew wild animals could be dangerous. What if it was a moose with big antlers? What would he do? What if it was a cougar hiding in the trees?

He crept closer to Grandma. Her eyes searched the tall grasses and willow bushes ahead, watching for movement.

Without warning, a giant grizzly reared up before them on the trail. Lawrence had never seen anything that big. The bear was as tall as their house.

The grizzly towered over them, grunting and snorting. His huge front paws were raised high. Lawrence knew from the elders that this was a bad sign. Bears were most dangerous when they stood up, especially grizzly bears. The elders also said that to run from a grizzly was certain death.

Instantly, Grandma threw her packsack in front of the grizzly. For a moment the bear hesitated, curious at what he had found.

Grandma hissed, "Whatever you do, Lawrence, don't move."

Ever so slowly, she raised her little rifle with its single bullet. She stared straight at the powerful beast. She knew she would not have a chance to reload.

Then she shot.

In slow motion, the grizzly began to fall toward them. Grandma jumped back, bumping into Lawrence as the giant bear toppled forward, crashing at their feet. A cloud of dust rose around them.

Almost not daring to breathe, they stared at the mountain of brown fur. Even lying down, it was as tall as Lawrence. The bear's claws were longer than Papa's fingers.

Were they really safe? Or would the bear jump up and chase them?

"If he moves, run and climb a tree as fast as you can," whispered Grandma.

"I'm not leaving you, Kokom."

"Don't worry. I'll be right behind you."

After a long time, Grandma sat down beside the bear. "Thank you for giving up your spirit and not killing us," she said.

"Thank you, grizzly bear," Lawrence repeated.

"This grizzly was the king of this area for a long time," said Grandma. "He is the biggest grizzly I've ever seen." She gave Lawrence a hug.

They hurried back to camp. On the way, Whiskers came slinking out of the bush.

"Come here, you scaredy rabbit," Grandma scolded. "I should have called you Wapoose after all. You never even barked once to warn us."

CAMP was abuzz with talk of the giant grizzly.
While Grandma rested, Papa, Uncle Louis and Uncle James went into the bush with the horses to bring back the bear. When he saw it, Uncle Louis was amazed.

"There are many bears in this area, but none as big as this one," he said.

They cut the meat into portions and loaded it on the horses. Back at the camp, it would be smoked and dried, then shared with all the families.

Every part of the bear could be used. Bear grease was prized as a rub for people with sore bones. The claws and teeth were given as gifts of honor. The hide made a prized rug.

While everyone worked, Grandma sat calmly, sipping her mug of tea under the shade of a tarp.

Papa joked, "Kokom, imagine what you could do with a slingshot."

More than once, Mama hugged Lawrence.

"My son," she said, "we will celebrate your bravery with a feast when we get home."

Something like a frog jumped in Lawrence's throat. He was so happy he wanted to cry.

Soon it was time to pack for home. The two families had worked hard, picking sacks of berries, smoking and drying meat for winter, and gathering large bundles of wild mint and medicine plants.

For the last time, Lawrence and his cousins swam in the cool, clear river.

"I'm a grizzly bear," shouted Lawrence. He snorted and splashed water everywhere. The children's laughter carried all the way to the camp.

L AWRENCE ran into the shed. Ooh-Hoo was not there. He ran out again, calling for Maruk.

"Where is Ooh-Hoo?" he asked breathlessly.

She burst into tears. "He flew away."

Lawrence ran to Papa. "Ooh-Hoo's gone," he cried.

Papa was unloading the wagon. "I told you that one day Ooh-Hoo would leave us," he said. "But don't worry. He's still too young to hunt for himself. After he practices flying some more, he'll be back for his supper."

Feeling lost, Lawrence wandered down to the woods. Suddenly, a dark shape sailed silently through the air.

"Ooh-Hoo!" Lawrence hollered. The owl settled on a nearby tree.

"Ooh-Hoo, I'm home."

The owl's head swiveled right around as if to listen better.

"I knocked over a giant grizzly bear, bigger than the shed. You don't have to be afraid of anything when I'm around," Lawrence bragged.

With a swoop, Ooh-Hoo flew into the boy's arms.

All day long, good smells came from the house as the family prepared for the gathering. As the guests arrived, Lawrence was surprised that he had so many aunts and uncles and cousins.

"Tell us about the grizzly bear," his cousins begged.

Finally the feast was ready. The table was covered with pots of moose stew and piles of fresh-baked bread. Special foods like smoked fish and duck soup were cooked in honor of the elders and storytellers. Lawrence ate until he was stuffed.

After supper, everyone settled comfortably outside on blankets around the fire. The storytelling began.

Uncle Louis stood up. He was tall and handsome. Everyone knew that he was the best storyteller around. Even the youngest children were quiet.

Uncle Louis stroked his bushy moustache before speaking.

"Once there was a man who walked in the four directions. He went north, south, east and west. He was a brave and seeking person who went from village to village learning all there was to know.

"He learned about new foods and how to cook them. In the prairies, he lived in tepees. In the cold lands, he lived in igloos.

"He saw waves of grass where the buffalo roamed. He tasted salty water where the sun rises and the sun sets. He came to dry lands where the sands were hot."

Lawrence saw himself in Uncle Louis's story, walking every step of the way.

Then it was Auntie Rose's turn. She told them about three hunters who surprised a grizzly bear eating their moose.

"The hunters climbed high into the only tree around. It wasn't very big or very strong. It started sagging until they were over the grizzly's head. The bear took a swipe at them, but the hunters were just out of reach. They hung down from that tree like berries thick on a branch. They looked tasty, too."

Auntie Rose turned to Uncle Dave. "Weren't you one of those hunters?" she asked.

"Oh, I was too skinny to tempt the bear," Uncle Dave replied. "But you should have seen my cousin Otamuwin. He was sorry he had eaten so much. The bear was drooling at the sight of him." Everyone laughed.

Grandpa rose and called Lawrence to his side. "This is my grandson. Not many boys his age meet a grizzly bear or care for an owl. From now on, we will call him Oskiniko."

The name meant Young Man. Lawrence stood proudly beside his grandpa.

The firelight flickered on Grandpa's gentle face. "This land has always given us what we need to live," he said gravely. "Like they told us long ago, as long as the rivers flow, this land is ours. It is up to all of us to care for it. Now it's your turn, grandchildren. The future is in your hands."

The stories continued long into the night. Lawrence's eyes began to droop. Soon he fell asleep listening to the familiar voices.

LAWRENCE rose early. He wanted to walk through the bush to his favorite places. He had heard many things around the fire. Now he wanted time to remember the stories and teachings.

As his hand touched the door, Mama whispered, "Oskiniko, you take care."

"I will, Mama." He slipped out to watch the earth wake again.

Ooh-Hoo hooted and followed Lawrence from tree to tree.

He is speaking especially to me, thought Lawrence.

By a little lake, he saw two ducks rising swiftly from the water. He knew that soon they would fly south for the winter.

At Prairie Creek, he went to his secret patch of chokecherry bushes. He picked a handful of the black berries to eat. They were sweet and juicy now. At the swimming hole, he went for a swim.

When he returned home, the sun was high in the sky. Mama and Grandma sat in the kitchen. They looked up sadly as he came in.

"Is something wrong?" Lawrence asked.

"I was waiting for you, my son," Mama said. "Tell the children to come in. I have something to tell all of you."

The children gathered around the kitchen table. Mama put fresh buns in front of them. Each child took one, then looked at her with questioning eyes.

"In a couple of days, they are going to come to take you to a school far away."

Maruk began to cry. "I don't want to go," she said.

Little brother Buddy and baby Leonard cried, too.

Lawrence spoke in a shaky voice. "You mean we're not going to live at home anymore?"

Mama's eyes were shiny with tears. "They told us there is nothing we can do. All the children have to go to their school or the parents will be put in prison."

She tried to smile as big tears rolled down her face.

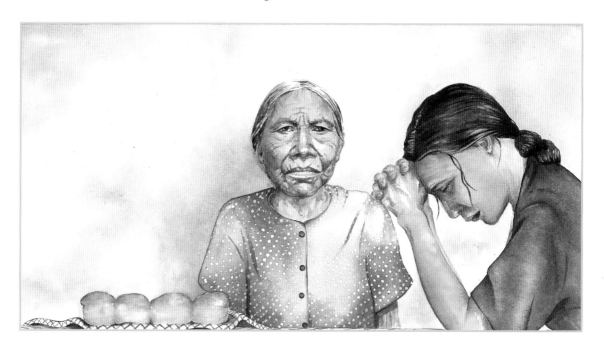

The children stared at their buns. No one felt hungry anymore.

Lawrence ran out of the house to the darkness of the shed. He held Ooh-Hoo close.

Home was the only place he knew. What would happen without Mama and Papa? What would he eat at the school? Where would he sleep? What would happen to his sister and brothers? Who would take care of Ooh-Hoo?

His tears fell on the bird's feathers.

THE day finally arrived. After breakfast, the children dressed in their best clothes. They stood close to Mama and Grandma. Grandpa put his arm around Grandma's shoulders.

A big brown truck with high sides pulled up. Two men got out. They both wore black and looked like giant crows.

"Hurry up," one of them said to the children loudly in English. "It's time to get on the truck."

The children pulled back, terrified of the strangers. Maruk clung to Mama's skirt.

Papa spoke to Lawrence in their own language.

"Be brave, Oskiniko. Take care of your younger sister and brothers."

The strange men lifted the crying children one by one onto the truck. Papa watched, his face angry, his fists clenched.

As the men closed up the back of the truck, Lawrence began to cry, too.

The sides of the truck were high. He couldn't see his family. He couldn't see Ooh-Hoo sitting in a tree.

As the truck pulled away, all Lawrence could see was the sky.

EPILOGUE

LAWRENCE (LARRY LOYIE) *was one of tens of thousands of North American native children who were taken from their families to residential schools during a hundred-year period that began around 1880. Some children were as young as two years old.*

In these schools, also called Indian boarding schools, mission schools and industrial schools in the United States and Canada, children were separated from their families for a long time. If they spoke their native language, the teachers washed their mouths with soap or strapped them. Parents who tried to keep their children at home could be put in jail.

Lawrence was ten years old when he was taken to St. Bernard's Mission residential school in northern Alberta. The children worked hard at St. Bernard's. They piled wood, planted fields of potatoes, darned and sewed their own clothes, washed laundry, cleaned floors and worked in

First Nations children call many people grandparents. They learn from all of them. Lawrence's mosoom (grandfather) Edward Twin lived to be 105 years old. He was Lawrence's mother's father. His kokom (grandmother) Bella Twin is famous for shooting one of the biggest grizzlies in North America. She was Lawrence's mother's aunt.

Photo courtesy Louise Loyie

Photo courtesy Roland Eben-Ebenau

Photo courtesy Eileen Kuhberg

Photo courtesy Eileen Kuhberg

Above: Being outdoors and traveling as a family with horses and wagon were an exciting part of Lawrence's childhood. After the family crossed a river (left), they would stop for lunch (right).

Below: Like other children who went to residential schools, Lawrence (circled) was not allowed to speak his native language. He was also made to learn Latin so he could be an altar boy at church.

Photo courtesy La société généalogique et historique de Smoky River, Donnelly, Alberta

the kitchen. There were many rules to follow every day, and the teachers were strict and even cruel. The children spent so little time in the classroom that many could not read or write when they left.

When Lawrence finally went home at age fourteen, he felt like a stranger. He tried to recapture the feeling of freedom he had felt when he lived with his family in the bush, but things were never the same. He left home and went to work on farms and in logging camps. Much later in life, he returned to school to learn English grammar. He taught himself how to type. That was his start at becoming a writer.

Although the residential schools no longer exist, many people still suffer from bad memories of those unhappy times. By talking about the past and by relearning their traditions, many First Nations people are now making efforts to heal the pain and to learn with pride about a beautiful and free way of life.

Lawrence's mother and nine of her children went to residential schools. This photo of younger sister Maruk (circled) was taken at her school.

Photo courtesy La société généalogique et historique de Smoky River, Donnelly, Alberta

Above: Lawrence's younger brothers Buddy (front row center) and Leonard (front row second from right) at residential school.

Below left: Children were brought to the residential schools from great distances. At St. Bernard's they went to church every day and lived in dormitories.

Below right: Lawrence looking at a grizzly bear in a museum in Kinuso in northern Alberta. The grizzly his grandmother shot was much bigger than this one.

Text copyright © 2002 by Lawrence A. Loyie and
Constance Brissenden
Photographs © 2002 by the owners
Illustrations copyright © 2002 by Heather D. Holmlund

First published in the USA in 2003
First paperback edition 2005
Eleventh paperback printing 2019

Groundwood Books / House of Anansi Press
groundwoodbooks.com

We gratefully acknowledge for their financial support of our
publishing program the Canada Council for the Arts, the Ontario
Arts Council and the Government of Canada.

Library and Archives Canada Cataloguing in Publication
Loyie, Larry
As long as the rivers flow: a last summer before residential school /
by Larry Loyie with Constance Brissenden; illustrated by Heather
D. Holmlund.
ISBN 978-0-88899-473-8 (bound)
ISBN 978-0-88899-696-1 (pbk.)
1. Loyie, Larry–Childhood and youth. 2. Cree Indians–Alberta–
Biography. 3. Authors, Canadian (English)–20th century–
Biography. I. Brissenden, Constance II. Holmlund, Heather D.
III. Title.
E99.C88L39 2002   971.23'004973   C2002-902190-1

Library of Congress Control Number: 2002106837

Book design by Michael Solomon
Printed and bound in China

 Canada Council   Conseil des Arts
for the Arts   du Canada

 ONTARIO ARTS COUNCIL
CONSEIL DES ARTS DE L'ONTARIO
an Ontario government agency
un organisme du gouvernement de l'Ontario

With the participation of the Government of Canada
Avec la participation du gouvernement du Canada | Canadä